This book
belongs to

....

D1465123

To George – my own little pixie

FREDERICK WARNE

Published by the Penguin Group
Penguin Books Ltd, 80 Strand, London WC2R 0RL, England
Penguin Young Readers Group, 345 Hudson Street,
New York, New York 10014, U.S.A.
Penguin Books Australia Ltd, 250 Camberwell Road, Camberwell,
Victoria 3124, Australia
Canada, India, New Zealand, South Africa

1 3 5 7 9 10 8 6 4 2

ISBN-13: 978 07232 5817 9
ISBN-10: 0 7232 5817 1

Printed in Great Britain

Wild Cherry Makes a Wish

by Pippa le Quesne

Welcome to the Flower Fairy Garden!

Where are the fairies?
Where can we find them?
We've seen the fairy-rings
They leave behind them!

Is it a secret
No one is telling?
Why, in your garden
Surely they're dwelling!

No need for journeying,
Seeking afar:
Where there are flowers,
There fairies are!

Contents

Chapter One
Wishes and Daydreams

'May I have this dance?' Beech asked, bowing low.

Wild Cherry Blossom felt like a princess as she took the handsome Tree Fairy's hand and let him lead her towards the dance floor. The waltz that the Flower Fairy orchestra had been playing ended and Wild Cherry was surprised to hear a very familiar tune

start up. If she wasn't mistaken, it was the soft, warbling song of a blackbird and not one usually heard at the seasonal ball. In fact, it was the same melody as the one that the blackbird who visited her each morning sang.

Wild Cherry opened her eyes and sighed. She was in her tree, and there, just at the end of the branch that she was curled up on, was her daily visitor announcing a new day. She had been dreaming.

The Tree Fairy yawned and stretched,

opening out her delicate pink wings
– jewelled with drops of dew that glistened
in the early morning sunshine. She always
got up at first light, but to make the most of
spring's precious days, she went to bed early
too. Wild Cherry loved this time of year
when her tree was covered in velvety leaves
and more clusters of pure white blossom
than she could count. The air all around her
was heavily scented with the promise of wild
cherries. They wouldn't arrive for a couple
of months yet, but the flowers, the leaves
and even the twigs carried their
perfume.

This morning, however, she was tired. The evening before, she'd attended the Spring Ball and stayed up late into the night. As always, it had been a magnificent occasion – a huge feast that everyone in Flower Fairyland had attended. The fairy court, hidden in a secret clearing in an overgrown patch of the garden, had been a spectacular sight – bustling with fairies in their most gorgeous outfits and lit by hundreds of firefly lanterns. And best of all had been the dancing.

Wild Cherry Blossom had spent the entire evening as close to the dance floor as possible. She'd chatted to all her friends and piled up an acorn bowl several times with mouth-watering fruit jelly and seed cake, but her eyes never left the light-footed fairies that whirled and twirled to the music. She loved dancing more than anything, yet, unlike in her dream, Wild Cherry never dared dance even a single step at one of the seasonal balls.

'If only I was more like Pansy,' the Tree Fairy murmured as she got herself ready for the day.

First of all, she folded up the moss blanket that she slept under and tucked it into a nook in the tree trunk. Then, she pulled out a twig comb from the pocket of her white dress and teased out the tangles from her wavy chestnut hair. Finally, she re-tied the red sash that she wore across her chest and fastened it in a bow at the back.

Like all the Flower Fairies, Wild Cherry Blossom was very pretty. Her cheeks were always rosy and she had a heart-shaped face, but she often let her hair fall across it, hiding her features. You see, although Wild Cherry had lots of friends, she was really very shy. She frequently visited the Garden Fairies and was not scared to venture out on to the marsh, but what she enjoyed most of all was sitting alone in her cherry tree, daydreaming.

'She's the best dancer I've ever seen!' Wild Cherry said out loud, swinging herself down to one of the lower branches where there was a good view of the woodland floor and she often did her thinking.

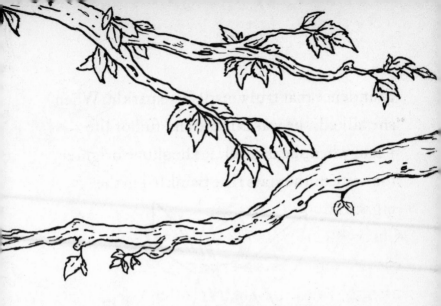

Pansy was a new arrival in Flower
Fairyland and everyone was talking about
how her flowers had cheered up the garden
after the long hard winter, blooming in
several brilliant colours. Wild Cherry had
seen her for the first time at the ball and
thought she was stunning. But it wasn't just
her bright dress – of purple, cream and blue
with a loud splash of yellow – that caught the
Tree Fairy's eye, or her petal-shaped wings
in the same wonderful colours, or even her
mass of springy golden curls. It was Pansy's

confidence that truly made her sparkle. When she talked, she was bubbly and full of life – and when she danced . . . she shone brighter than any of the stars that twinkled in the night sky.

She didn't put a foot wrong, Wild Cherry thought to herself as she picked a clump of blossom and began to absent-mindedly pluck the petals one by one. *If I knew all the steps, then I wouldn't be scared to dance in front of everyone, either*. She was sitting cross-legged and, as she let the petals fall into her skirt, she began to feel a little sad.

Wild Cherry remembered how, like all the Flower Fairies, she had learnt to dance when she was very young. She'd loved it from the start and had practised like mad every night before she went to bed. However, being a Tree Fairy, she also had climbing lessons and, one day, when she lost her balance and fell awkwardly, she'd injured a wing. Much to her dismay, it meant that she couldn't dance until it had completely healed and so she missed a whole series of classes where the other fairies learnt new steps.

Wild Cherry sighed for the second time that morning. *If only I wasn't so silly and shy*, she thought, scolding herself.

She knew very well that she should have asked for extra help when she'd recovered. But, instead, she'd hidden at the back of the class, struggling to keep up. And after that, although she never stopped dreaming about spinning her way around the dance floor, she wasn't brave enough to try.

The Tree Fairy shook her head to dismiss the thought and began looking for a leaf large enough to wrap up the petals she'd collected.

Just then, a flash of bright red caught her eye.

'A ladybird – to cheer me up!' Wild Cherry exclaimed.

It was quite unusual to set eyes on one so early in the year, as they like to sleep until the summer months, and in Flower Fairyland it was considered very lucky.

At that moment, the pretty beetle landed close enough for Wild Cherry to see each of its shiny black spots and she swiftly counted them, holding her breath in anticipation.

'Seven!' she cried out in delight. Seven spots entitled you to a wish! But you had to make it before the ladybird flew away.

Quick, quick, Wild Cherry thought to herself, as the ladybird spread its wings.

She squeezed her eyes shut, knowing precisely what she wanted more than anything. 'I wish . . .' she said eagerly. 'I wish . . . I wish I could learn to dance like Pansy!' And then she opened them at the precise moment that the ladybird launched itself into the air – whisking her wish away with it.

Chapter Two
The Dance Class

Pear Blossom was always cheerful. And he was always full of song. Wild Cherry loved spending the afternoon sitting in his tree, listening as he chattered away to the garden birds. He could imitate each of their melodies perfectly and his treetop was always busy with a chaffinch or thrush bringing their young to visit him or stopping by to catch up on Flower Fairy news.

Wild Cherry also felt incredibly at home surrounded by the clouds of white pear blossom and she often found herself talking about things that she never told anyone else. Soon after the last chaffinch had flown off to find some worms for his tea, the two Tree Fairies began to discuss the Spring Ball and it wasn't long before Wild Cherry had shared her secret.

'You know, I've never noticed that you don't actually dance at the seasonal balls!' Pear Blossom sounded amazed. 'I thought that was practically all you did!'

'No,' replied Wild Cherry, her cheeks tinged pink. 'I just spend all my time by the dance floor, watching.'

'Well,' said Pear, in a good-natured way, 'we can soon change that.'

Without another word he jumped from his perch and, beckoning to his friend to follow him, flew down to the very lowest bough of the pear tree. Once there, he sat astride a branch and waited until Wild Cherry landed next to him. She was about to ask him what they were doing when he held up one hand to silence her and then cupped the other behind his pointy elf-like ear.

'Ah, good, just as I thought,' Pear Blossom said, suddenly leaning forward so that his head disappeared through the foliage. Wild Cherry Blossom was puzzled by her friend's behaviour, but she sat still and listened intently. And then, there it was – the sound of Flower Fairies singing. Gradually, it got louder until she could quite clearly hear the words:

'Lavender's blue, dilly dilly,
    Lavender's green;
When you are king , dilly dilly,
    I shall be queen'

as she peered down to find out where it was coming from, the two Crocus Fairies, followed by Daffodil, Candytuft and Tulip came into view – waving Canterbury bells and dancing as they sang. Or rather, they were trying to dance as best they could but mainly they were skipping along. They were obviously enjoying themselves though and didn't seem remotely self-conscious. As they linked hands and formed a circle around the trunk of the pear tree, a solo voice could be heard singing the rest of the verse:

'Who told you so, dilly dilly,
 Who told you so?
Twas my own heart, dilly dilly,
 That told me so'

As the dancers joined in the chorus, out from behind the rockery came an older

Flower Fairy moving in time to the music with grace and ease. It was Pansy!

Pear Blossom sat upright and beamed at Wild Cherry. 'I thought it was the right time of day for Pansy's dance lesson. You must join in, of course!'

Then,
much to
Wild Cherry's
horror, before
she could stop
him, he called,
'Pansy! Pansy! We're up
here!'

The song had ended and his voice
rang out, causing the Garden Fairy to look
up and wave.

'Oh, P-Pear . . .' Wild Cherry Blossom
stuttered. 'I couldn't possibly . . .'

But it was too late. Pansy was turning away
from her class and it was obvious that she
was about to come and join the Tree Fairies to
find out what Pear Blossom wanted.

The Woodland Fairy was suddenly
overwhelmed by shyness. It wasn't that she
didn't want to make friends with Pansy . . .

she just felt very foolish that she'd spent all this time wishing she could dance and hiding the fact that she couldn't.

'Afternoon, Pansy,' Pear Blossom said warmly, as the Garden Fairy took off from the ground. 'This is my friend Wild Cherry.'

Pansy smiled broadly as she came to rest beside them. 'And what an afternoon it's been! I was so busy looking after my flowers that I nearly forgot the time and so had to rush to my dance class.' She burbled away, not in the least bit timid. 'Phew – I'm really thirsty. How about making us a cup of chamomile tea?'

'No problem at all,' Pear Blossom replied, getting up. 'Oh, and while I'm gone, Wild Cherry has got something to ask you.'

'Go on,' said Pansy, fixing her with a steady gaze.

Wild Cherry blushed fiercely. Her throat was really dry and she felt sure that she wouldn't be able to utter a single word. Without meaning to, she panicked and before she knew what she was saying, she squeaked, 'I've got to go!'

Then, she jumped to her feet and, forgetting the wish that she had made earlier that day, headed for home just as fast as her wings would carry her.

Chapter Three
Visiting

Wild Cherry Blossom had barely slept a wink. She was so ashamed of herself for having flown off like that. What would Pansy think – and poor old Pear, who was only trying to be kind.

I was rude and ungrateful and not at all as a Flower Fairy should be! she thought to herself, as she fluttered over the garden wall.

When Wild Cherry had finally given up trying to get any more rest, she decided to go and apologize to Pansy straight after breakfast. She'd been too nervous to eat more than a handful of dried berries but it was a beautiful day and the sight of the clear blue sky gave her energy.

It was some distance from the woodland to the garden and the Tree Fairy's wings were quite sore from her frantic flight the day before, so Wild Cherry started walking just as soon as she could. She guessed that Pansy's patch would be where the bravest Garden

Fairies tended to live – in the flower bed that bordered the humans' lawn – and set off in that direction.

As she went, she reminded herself just how important manners were and that this time, when she came across the confident Garden Fairy, she would just have to overcome her shyness. *Anyway, she seemed very friendly – and she might not have thought what I did was as bad as all that ...*

She was busily telling herself this as she made her way towards the front of the flower bed and so got a tremendous shock when she parted the long thin grape hyacinth leaves. There, just a stone's throw away, was Pansy, standing boldly

on the edge of the lawn, talking loudly to
Dandelion. Wild Cherry's heart immediately
began to beat faster.

The Tree Fairy already knew Dandelion
well enough. He was full of mischief and
an impish smile never left his lips. In fact,
everything about his appearance was lively.
The sleeves of his tunic and his shorts were
cheerful stripes of gold and green – the same
colour as his wings – and he had playful
pompoms on his shoes.

'So how was your afternoon? Did your class go well?' he was asking Pansy. He hopped from foot to foot as he spoke, as if he found it difficult to stay still for more than a moment. Dandelion was also an enthusiastic dancer.

'Oh, it was great!' Pansy replied. 'But a strange thing happened afterwards...'

Wild Cherry Blossom's heart missed a beat.

'Pear was watching and he had a friend of his with him – Wild Cherry...'

She's going to tell him what happened and how strangely I behaved, the Tree Fairy thought to herself.
I just can't bear it!

'Go on,' said Dandelion, sounding intrigued.

Suddenly, making friends was the last thing on Wild Cherry's mind. She felt so embarrassed! At that moment, all she wanted was to be in her own private spot in the woodlands. So, without waiting to hear what Pansy actually had to say, she scurried back the way she had come, not stopping to talk to anyone as she went.

* * *

Wild Cherry Blossom would probably have spent the rest of the day sitting in her tree, thinking. Although deep down she was very disappointed with how things had turned out, she was trying to convince herself that it was probably for the best.

'After all, I don't even know if I can dance any more,' she said out loud. 'At least this way there's still hope. I mean, just imagine if I found out that I was terrible at it – then I couldn't even dream about being a dancer!'

Once she'd reached this conclusion she

began to feel a bit better. So much so, that when Bluebell called up to her to ask if she was going out in the fields that afternoon and if she could take a message to Heart's-ease for him, she agreed.

When Bluebell's flowers blossomed, they spread out like a huge carpet across the woodland floor. So he was kept very busy tending to them and could always be found somewhere among their nodding blue heads. Knowing this, the thrushes would often use him as a drop-off point for messages that

they were delivering from the garden. Then
either the Wild Flower Fairies would come
and ask if he had any letters for them or he
would beg a favour from a passing fairy to
take them further afield.

Wild Cherry's mood was much lighter
as she made her way along a deep rut in the
field where Heart's-ease lived. She soon
spotted him sitting cross-legged on the
freshly ploughed earth, scribbling away in
his notebook. He too was a solitary kind of
fairy who spent a lot of time with his head

buried in a book – either reading or filling a diary with his thoughts. Unlike Wild Cherry, though, he rarely ventured to the garden and mainly caught up with the goings-on from those that visited his corner of Flower Fairyland.

'Hello, Heart's-ease,' Wild Cherry called. 'I hope I'm not disturbing you.'

The Wild Flower Fairy looked up. 'My dear friend! Not at all!'

Heart's-ease put down his quill pen and indicated for Wild Cherry to sit down next to him. 'So what brings you this way – it's been ages!'

'I know – but it's great to see you.' The Tree Fairy felt very affectionately towards Heart's-ease, as they had a lot in common.

'Can I get you a drink – jasmine tea perhaps?' he asked her.

'Oh yes, please,' she replied. Then remembering the letter she was carrying, Wild Cherry held it out. 'This is for you from the garden – Bluebell asked me to deliver it.'

Heart's-Ease, who clearly didn't receive many letters, forgot all about their drinks and eagerly broke the seal on the folded sycamore leaf.

'Well, I never!' he exclaimed. 'What an afternoon this is turning out to be. First of all the pleasure of your company, then an unexpected letter – and now, a very special fairy arriving for tea!'

'How lovely,' Wild Cherry said sincerely, wondering who the surprise visit was from. Judging by her friend's enthusiasm, she guessed it might be the Queen of the Meadows or even Kingcup.

'Oh, Wild Cherry – I'm ever so pleased. It's my cousin from the garden, whom I've never yet met. She's coming out here to see me!'

Heart's-ease was now dashing back and forth – picking up his notebook one minute, organizing tea things the next and getting himself in quite a fluster. The Woodland

Fairy was gently amused. She had never
seen him in such a state – ordinarily he was
very calm and never in a hurry. His curly
hair seemed to have taken on a life of its own
and the more he pushed it out of his eyes or
tried to smooth it back, the more wiry and
troublesome it became. Heart's-ease did
look funny with it standing up from his head!
Suppressing a giggle, Wild Cherry decided
that she should lend a hand.

'I'll help you get ready, Heart's-ease. Now tell me precisely – who is coming to tea?'

Heart's-ease stopped what he was doing and took a couple of deep breaths. 'Oh, it's marvellous, Wild Cherry . . . She's only just arrived in Flower Fairyland . . . And of course, you must join us. I'd love you to meet my cousin.'

'But you haven't told me who she is!' Wild Cherry laughed.

'Silly me.' The Wild Flower Fairy grinned. 'Why – it's Pansy, of course!'

They couldn't be more different, Wild Cherry Blossom thought to herself.

Pansy's dress was a bold statement, whereas Hearts-ease's clothes were a more delicate design, and his wings were made up of intricate patterns as opposed to the vibrant splashes of colour on hers. It seemed that the Garden Fairy was always chirpy and energetic in contrast to the Wild Fairy who preferred to be quiet and still.

But they get on really well. Wild Cherry mulled this over as she watched the two cousins, talking and laughing and having a splendid time.

When she'd discovered that Pansy was the mysterious visitor, the Tree Fairy hastily made her excuses to Heart's-ease – mumbling something about needing to get home. However, as she said goodbye to her friend, she couldn't ignore the sinking feeling in the pit of her stomach. She was well aware that the situation with Pansy was going from bad to worse and she knew that she wouldn't be able to avoid her forever. Yet she hoped that time might work its wonders and once the memory of the silliness of the day before had faded, then it would be much easier to approach the Garden Fairy.

Wild Cherry had just left Heart's-ease and was clambering through the hedgerow, when the sound of Pansy arriving stopped her in her tracks. Staying very still, she listened as the cousins exchanged greetings before settling down to tea. She was about to set off again but instead, like a moth drawn to a light, parted the leaves at the front of the hedgerow to take another peek at Pansy.

That was where Wild Cherry was now, thinking to herself how surprising life could be – what with two fairies as different as chalk and cheese getting on so well. She didn't know how long she'd been crouching there, but as she tried for the umpteenth time to get comfortable amidst the spiky twigs, Pansy announced that it was time for her to go.

'It was brilliant to meet you, cousin,' the Garden Fairy said, giving Heart's-ease a kiss on the cheek. 'Now you make sure you come and visit me some time soon.'

'Oh, I will,' he replied, blushing to the roots of his hair. 'Goodbye.'

Pansy turned around to wave as she picked her way down the ploughed field and when Wild Cherry heard Heart's-ease sigh contentedly to himself, she felt very pleased for her friend. In the distance Pansy could be heard humming loudly as she walked and, curiosity getting the better of her, Wild Cherry Blossom found herself following.

Pansy was happily singing the same folk song as the day before and when she reached the verse that fitted her surroundings perfectly she whooped in delight and began to dance.

'Call up your friends, dilly, dilly,
Set them to work,
Some to the plough, dilly dilly,
Some to the fork.'

Each time there was a 'dilly dilly', the athletic fairy kicked up both her legs in the air, causing her to leave the ground for a split second and giggle with pleasure.

'Some to the hay, dilly dilly,
Some to thresh corn,
Whilst you and I, dilly dilly,
Keep ourselves warm.'

Pansy spun round and round, her floaty dress fanning out around her. Then she skipped along for a few steps before bounding elegantly. Each time she jumped she seemed to propel herself higher and further forward, making it look as if it was the easiest thing in the world.

Wild Cherry was utterly absorbed – she had never seen anything so wonderful in all her life. And so when the earth began to tremble beneath her feet, she didn't take much notice. *It must be Pansy's dancing that's making the ground shake*, she thought casually.

When the performance finally came to an end, the Garden Fairy collapsed in a heap, completely breathless. It was then that it dawned on Wild Cherry – not only could she still feel the vibrations beneath her feet, but they were getting stronger. She had crept along behind Pansy keeping just out of sight

but
now,
sensing
danger, she
instinctively
shot up into the
nearest tree. And it
didn't take her a second to see
what was causing the tremors . . .

Humans! Wild Cherry gasped, a shiver
running down her spine. *And they're
coming this way!*

She glanced down at Pansy and
was about to call out to her to
fly up into the tree when
she realized that the
Garden Fairy still hadn't
caught her breath. She

would never have the strength to make the distance and, as she wasn't a Tree Fairy, she might not be good enough at climbing to reach the safety of the top branches.

Boom, boom, boom! Wild Cherry's whole universe seemed to be shaking now as the children ran along in the precise direction of where Pansy was sprawled out on the path. She was in real danger of being discovered – or worse still – trampled! Wild Cherry was going to have to do something to save her, and fast!

Chapter Five
To the Rescue!

Desperate for ideas, Wild Cherry looked
frantically about her.

The tree that she had flown into was an elm
and she wondered if its Flower Fairy was
at home. *I daren't shout out in case the humans
hear me*, she thought, quickly scanning the
branches for any sign of him. The leaves were
dark green and would make him difficult to
spot in his similarly coloured clothes,
unless of course he was sitting
among the blossom. Wild
Cherry was squinting
at the tiny clusters of
flowers, in a last-ditch
attempt to find help,

when she had a sudden flash of inspiration.

She would create a diversion! As there wasn't time to move Pansy, the only thing to do was to distract the children and lead them in a different direction. Wild Cherry rummaged around in the deep pockets of her dress – yup, she had what she needed. Taking a deep breath, she opened her wings.

'It's now or never!' she said, leaping into the air.

The two girls had slowed to a walk but nonetheless they were only twenty strides or so away. When Wild Cherry reached them, she hovered behind them and delved a hand into her pocket. Taking out a pinch of ground-up pollen, she threw it up into the air and whispered, 'Fairy dust, fairy dust, bring me a breeze!'

Instantly, a warm current of wind began to pick up. *This might just work!* the Tree

Fairy thought, as she carefully unfolded
the cherry tree leaf that she'd produced
from her other pocket. Then, plucking up
her courage, she shook the contents of the
purse at the children, getting as close as she
could without being seen. At first the white
blossom began to cascade to the ground but
the next moment the breeze had caught the
petals and slowly but surely they began to
dance and whirl like snowflakes.

At first, Wild Cherry thought that the

girls hadn't noticed, but suddenly one of them cried out.

'Janet, look – it's snowing!' she said, coming to a halt and pointing to the flurry of blossom.

'Oh, wow!' exclaimed the shorter girl, her pretty face breaking into an enormous grin.

'Hang on a minute,' said her friend, holding out an upturned hand. 'These aren't snowflakes – they're petals!'

Yes! The Tree Fairy had successfully gained their interest and so far they hadn't spotted her.

However, she knew that her job was only half done. Taking the remaining sprinkling of fairy dust from her pocket, she blew it off her hand, sending a dart of air into the midst of the swirling blossom. After a moment or two, the petal cloud began to move away from the children.

Wild Cherry retreated to the safety of a nearby tree and held her breath. Then, as she had hoped, the two mesmerized girls began to chase after the cloud – on a completely different course to the one that led them to Pansy.

* * *

'I did it, I actually did it!'

If Wild Cherry Blossom had even a tiny bit of energy left, she would have jumped for joy.

Five minutes or so had passed since she'd watched the children disappear into the distance and they were no longer visible on the horizon. By the time that Wild Cherry had flown into the uppermost branches to hide, there was no sign of Pansy. She just couldn't believe how well things had turned out. In fact she couldn't remember the last time she'd felt such a thrill of success.

The sun was beginning to set and the Tree
Fairy gazed at the rich orange and yellows
melting across the afternoon sky. What a
view it was from the giddy heights of a tall
elm! She chuckled to herself. *There was a time
when I was too scared to sit at the top of a tree*, she
recalled.

It was true – not so long ago she had been a nervous climber, until the day that baby Apple Blossom scrambled up too high and needed rescuing. Wild Cherry scratched her head. *That's twice now that I've been unexpectedly brave.*

She sat very still for a minute, lost in thought.

'On both occasions,' she said aloud, 'rather than worrying that I might fail, I just did something without thinking and it turned out all right.'

All of a sudden the Tree Fairy got up from her resting place. 'There's just one more thing I'd like to do while I remember how this feels …' And summoning her remaining strength, she launched herself purposefully into the air.

Chapter Five
Hooray for Wild Cherry

Wild Cherry was concentrating so hard on carefully lowering herself down the garden wall that she hadn't heard the commotion behind her.

I don't think I've ever felt so tired, she thought to herself, her eyelids drooping. It had been a long day for the Woodland Fairy and she yearned to be tucked up in her tree. Not only had she survived on very little sleep but it had been such an eventful day!

The energy that she'd felt when she first left the elm tree had been used up by the sheer effort of keeping herself in the air. Long before she reached the garden, her wings had given up and now she was faced with the strenuous task of climbing down the wall.

Clap, clap, clap, clap!

'OK. Right foot, left arm, left foot, right arm,' Wild Cherry instructed herself as she went. 'Nearly there now . . .'

Clap, clap, clap, clap!

'What on earth is that?' she wondered aloud, but didn't dare look round for fear of losing her balance.

A moment later her feet touched the ground and she immediately swung about to see where the strange noise was coming from.

Wild Cherry got such a jolt from the sight that met her eyes, that she nearly fell over.

For there, standing in a semi-circle and all clapping rhythmically, were Pear Blossom, Dandelion, Zinnia, Tulip and Pansy! And before she could utter a single word, Pear Blossom stepped forward.

'Three cheers for Wild Cherry Blossom. Hip hip hooray!' shouted her old friend, and the others joined in.

'Hip hip hooray! Hip hip hooray!'

'W-what's going on?' she asked, feeling quite dazed and utterly confused.

'I was up at the top of my tree . . . and I saw what you did . . . you were so brave! I mean to say, I know that you saved Pansy. We all do!' the words tumbled out of Pear.

Wild Cherry stared down at her shoes to avoid his eyes. All the Garden Fairies were talking at once now but she was busy trying to stop her cheeks from burning with embarrassment. Then one voice spoke, clear above the others.

'Thank you so much.'

It was Pansy!

Wild Cherry gulped. And then, the resolve that she'd felt earlier came back to her and she looked up and met Pansy's gaze.

'I'm sorry about yesterday,' she said, talking slowly so as not to stutter. 'It wasn't that I didn't want to be friends with you...' She took a deep breath. 'It's just that I'm shy.'

'Oh, don't worry.' Pansy beamed at her. 'I was telling Dandelion all about it – only because I was worried that I'd done something wrong – and he explained that you can be a bit quiet sometimes.'

So she didn't think I was awful! Wild Cherry breathed a sigh of relief. It had just been a ridiculous misunderstanding.

'Actually,' the Tree Fairy said, suddenly not feeling in the least bit nervous, 'I wanted to ask you something.' And she glanced at Pear Blossom, who gave her a knowing grin and, without further ado, ushered the others away.

'Will you let me go

first?' Pansy asked, putting an arm about her shoulder and leading her over to a couple of mushroom stools.

Wild Cherry nodded, at the same time gratefully sinking into the cushioned seat.

'Well,' said the Garden Fairy, 'you really got me out of a sticky situation this afternoon. So, I want to thank you. Is there anything – anything at all that I can do to repay you?'

'I can't dance!' Wild Cherry blurted out. 'And I want to learn – only I'm scared that I might not be any good at it.'

Pansy chuckled. 'Don't be daft! Of course you would. Anyway, that's what dance classes are for! I mean, you saw Daff and Tulip and the rest of them – they're not experts yet – but they're learning, and they're really enjoying themselves.'

It was true – none of them had looked brilliant but they were obviously keen to learn. Wild Cherry suddenly realized that she wasn't the only Flower Fairy who needed some practice. She had nothing to worry about after all.

'Besides – you're not short of courage,' the Garden Fairy went on. 'What you did to distract those children was really brave!'

Wild Cherry smiled. 'I guess so . . .'

'I've got it!' Pansy announced, looking pleased with herself. 'What I'll do to repay you is give you some private lessons. And by the time the Summer Ball comes along you'll be one of the best dancers in Flower Fairyland.

'Now, I won't take no for an answer.' She leant across and patted Wild Cherry kindly on the arm. 'Listen, it's getting late and I for one am starving. Come on. Pear Blossom has invited us all to supper. Race you there!'

Pansy winked at her and Wild Cherry found herself blushing – but this time it was with pleasure.

Then, without another word, the energetic Garden Fairy sprang up from her seat and sped off.

Wild Cherry Blossom hung back for a moment and stared up at the dusky sky, trying to absorb everything that had just happened. Her wish had been granted! Finally, she would be able to dance at the fairy court. She twirled around, her arms outstretched.

'Thank you, ladybird – wherever you are!' she called into the darkness, and then, forgetting her tiredness, she skipped and danced so she could catch up with her new friend.

FLOWER
FAIRIES™
FRIENDS

Visit our Flower Fairies website at:

www.flowerfairies.com

There are lots of fun Flower Fairy games and
activities for you to play, plus you can find out more
about all your favourite fairy friends!

More tales from these Flower Fairies™ coming soon!

Buttercup

Almond Blossom

Candytuft

Strawberry